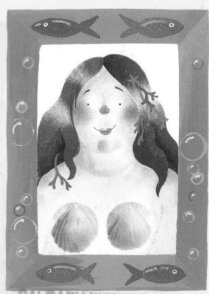

Copyright © 2012, 2013 by Lemniscaat, Rotterdam, The Netherlands
First published in The Netherlands under the title *Bij ons in de straat*
Text copyright © 2012 by Koos Meinderts
Illustration copyright © 2012 by Annette Fienieg
English translation copyright © 2013 by Lemniscaat USA LLC • New York
All rights reserved.

First published in the United States and Canada in 2012 by Lemniscaat USA LLC • New York
Distributed in the United States by Lemniscaat USA LLC • New York

Library of Congress Cataloging-in-Publication Data is available.
ISBN 13: 978-1-935954-24-8 (Hardcover)
Printing and binding: Worzalla, Stevens Point, WI USA
First U.S. edition

Koos Meinderts & Annette Fienieg

ON MY STREET

Adapted by MaryChris Bradley

LEMNISCAAT

Come along with me and meet,

All the people on my street.

Some are strange and some are lazy,

Some are silly and some are crazy!

Her house is large and painted green,

And inside it you'll find a Queen.

With royal ears and regal chin,

She always wears a noble grin.

NUMBER TWO – 'LIGHTFINGERS' LOUIE

Here lives a thief, who's very picky,

And though his fingers are quite sticky,

When he goes outside to steal,

He only takes the stuff that's real.

NUMBER THREE – MS. ARA BESQUE

A dancer lives at number three,

She floats on air just like a bee.

On many stages has she danced,

From circus tent to Paris, France!

NUMBER FOUR – CHARLIE NOBLE

Though his house looks like a boat,

I doubt that it ever would float,

But that's a thought he wouldn't think,

For he has named it—Never Sink.

Next we stop and spend some hours,

In a house, topped off with towers,

Having scones and sipping tea,

With our new friend Mr. Cree.

NUMBER SIX – 'SIX-SHOOTER' JAMES

A cowboy lives at Number Six,

Roping hogs and doing tricks,

But after shooting his own hat,

He's put an end to all of that.

Our Auntie, named Fritzi MacFluff,

Lives with her kitties, Sniffy and Snuff.

Her house is all knitted from yarn,

But you'll find she gives not a darn!

NUMBER EIGHT – ED TOTTLES

This rickety house that's said to be haunted,

Is really the home of a man often taunted,

For the owner, the odd Mr. Tottles,

Has filled it with old empty bottles!

Merry Maide loves all things with fins,

From whales to sardines in their tins.

It seems she's finally got her wish,

And now resides with her four fish.

NUMBER TEN – MR. COOK

Mr. Cook has a bistro or diner,

It's said there's no food that's finer,

But his guests, they must race to the table,

For he'll eat it all first, if he's able.

NUMBER ELEVEN – KOOS AND ANNETTE

The best house is last and it's mine,

Here I write poems I think are quite fine,

While downstairs is an artist at work,

Drawing neighbors and all of their quirks.

We hope that you've found this book fun,

But now sadly it seems, we are done!